Welcome to My Life with Joy! My name is Joy.

I'm so excited that you are here with me to experience the great joy that Jesus talks about in the Bible. On the next pages I'm going to introduce you to my 3 friends & sisters, Faith, Hope, & Grace. If you think about it, how can you experience great joy if you don't have Faith (Faith in God), Hope (hope in everlasting life), & Grace (God's grace) in your life? That's why I invited them to my book! We are all so happy to have you join us in this oh so very joyful book about JOY!!

Hi! I'm Faith
Have Faith in God

These are my friends & sisters! Faith, Hope, & Grace!

Hi! I'm Hope
Hope in salvation

Hi! I'm Grace
The Grace of God

Romans 15:13

May the God of hope fill you with all joy and peace as you trust in him, so that you may overflow with hope by the power of the Holy Spirit.

If you really get to know God, you will find He is full of hope. The Holy Spirit will bring peace to your soul if you just trust Him! Knowing that, you should be restful, knowing that God will take care of everything! Be Joyful! God is good & great!

Psalm 28:7

The Lord is my strength and shield; my heart trusts in him, and he helps me. My heart leaps for joy and with my song I praise him.

God loves it when you praise Him and sing songs of praise to Him. You can trust Him & know He will protect you & give you strength to face your fears. He will always be there for you. Be joyful!

Proverbs 16:20

Those who listen to instruction will prosper; those who trust the Lord will be joyful.

If you do what God asks you to do (which is always the right thing) & follow the 10 Commandments the best you could, God will lead you on a great & amazing journey! Trust God, He is full of truth & love, and He will guide you through life's great adventures!

1 Peter 1:8

You love him even though you have never seen him. Though you do not see him now, you trust him; and you rejoice with a glorious, inexpressible joy.

Isn't it funny how even though you can't see God, you just "know" He is there & you can even trust Him with your life. You can feel Him in your heart. That's the Holy Spirit in you. Sometimes I want to just jump up & down & right off of this page because He fills my life with such joy!!!

Psalms 16:11

You make known to me the path of life; you will fill me with joy in your presence, with eternal pleasures at your right hand.

If you follow God, He will lead you in the right direction. He has your whole life planned out for you. He is always going to be there for you every step of the way.

Romans 12:12

Be joyful in hope, patient in affliction, faithful in prayer.

Let's talk about patience. God's timing is perfect. So when your praying for something, or calling out to God for help, be patient, He is listening. He may be waiting for a more perfect time. He also decides what is best for you. He will see you through & He is right there with you. Trust Him.

Psalm 94:19

When I am filled with cares, Your comfort brings me joy.

God wants you to take His hand & walk with Him. He will even carry you the rest of the way to see you through life's scary times. He is there to comfort you when you are sad & feeling lonely. He loves you so much! He weeps when you weep. Take comfort in God, He wants you to reach out to Him when your feeling troubled.

Psalm 30:5

Weeping may last through the night, but joy comes with the morning.

The sad times never last very long. Before you know it your laughing again! God will get you through those tough times, & before you know it, it's over. And because of Jesus, we have everlasting life where there will be no more weeping or sadness.

For the Lord your God is living among you. He is a mighty savior. He will take delight in you with gladness. With his love, he will calm all your fears. He will rejoice over you with joyful songs.

Zephaniah 3:17

Bring Joy

The Holy Spirit produces this kind of fruit in our lives: love, JOY, peace, patience, kindness, goodness, faithfulness, gentleness, and self-control.

Galatians 5:22-23

Psalm 47:1

Come, everyone! Clap your hands! Shout to God with joyful praise!

Share what you know & learned about Jesus with your friends. There are so many great stories in the Bible to share with them too. Invite them to church with you. It's so awesome to make new friendships isn't it? Why not introduce Jesus to your friends?

About the Author

I was unable to have children and lost my
husband of 26 years in a motorcycle accident.
It was at that time when my walk with Christ
began & I decided to adopt a child from foster
care. My little girl is the inspiration of this
series of books & my desire to start writing
children's books. I am an Artist & also love to
write, so I put the two together. I am a
Christian & love my God dearly. I think kids
need to know Christ & know what the Bible is
all about. You can visit my website & check
out my art, books, & poetry.

www.carlacarson.com